Family Matters

Written by Joanna Nadin

Illustrated by Kübra Teber

Chapter 1: Teatime Torment

Harvey Parks and Luka Duric had three things in common.

(1) They were eight years old.

(2) They were boys.

(3) And they were in the same class at Bingley Primary School.

But that's where the things they had in common ended.

While Harvey liked to play football in the park, Luka liked to stay inside and read.

When Harvey was climbing trees and fighting imaginary dragons, Luka was playing computer games or figuring out code on his computer.

Though Harvey was happy getting messy in the garden with his mum, Luka preferred to bake cakes in the kitchen with his dad, and they always cleaned up afterwards.

Harvey and Luka were as different as a peach and a peanut, and thought it would be pointless trying to get to know each other.

So, in class, they always talked to other people.

At break time, they played with different friends.

And at home time, they always walked away from their school in opposite directions. Harvey went left with his mum, and Luka went right with his dad, until one wet Wednesday when the unthinkable happened. The boys trooped out of class to find their parents chatting under the same umbrella.

"What's going on?" said Luka.

"No idea," said Harvey.

"Luka's dad has invited us over for tea," said Ms Parks to Harvey. "Isn't that nice?"

"Um … I suppose so," replied Harvey.

"But I was going to work on some code," Luka said to his dad.

"Well, Harvey can help you," said Mr Duric. "Won't that be fun?"

The boys looked at each other. It was just one teatime, wasn't it?

How bad could it be?

Chapter 2: From Bad to Worse

That wet Wednesday afternoon was bad. In fact, it was worse than they could have imagined.

Harvey messed up Luka's code, so Luka refused to go into the garden to play footie. Then Harvey ate the last cake (they were much nicer than the ones his mum made) even though Luka had wanted to keep it for his packed lunch the next day.

"How about I make us all another batch and you can come over again next Wednesday?" suggested Mr Duric.

Harvey couldn't think of anything he'd like to do less, even though the cakes were tempting. "I—" he began.

His mum interrupted him. "We'd love to," she said. "Thank you so much."

And they did. Next Wednesday turned into the Wednesday after that and the Wednesday after that until, one afternoon, a few months later, Mr Duric said he had an exciting announcement to make.

"I hope it's that this is the last tea together," thought Luka.

"No more boring code," hoped Harvey.

Unfortunately, they were both wrong.

"We're getting married!" exclaimed Luka's dad as he put his arm round Harvey's mum.

"Isn't it wonderful?" said Harvey's mum, and she gave the boys a wide smile.

"Wonderful?" they both said. "Are you joking?"

"I want it to be just you and me," said Luka later that evening. Because, even though his dad was scared of spiders and the dark, he was the best dad in the world.

"It'll all be brilliant," said Luka's dad. "You'll see."

And Harvey's mum might not be great at making cakes but she was the best mum in the world. "Can't we stay as we are?" asked Harvey. "We're fine, just the two of us, aren't we?"

"Don't you worry," said his mum. "Nothing will change."

But as they settled down in their beds that night, both boys felt far from fine and not even one teensy bit brilliant.

"This is going to be terrible," Harvey said to his bear, Kevin.

"It's going to be absolute rubbish," Luka said to his robot, Dave.

And it was.

Chapter 3: Fighting Like Cats and Dogs

First of all, Harvey and Luka couldn't agree on what flavour cake they should have at the wedding.

"I want chocolate cake!" yelled Harvey. "Chocolate is the best!"

"Lemon drizzle is the best!" Luka snapped back. "I want lemon drizzle or I'm not even coming."

So, in the end, they had a mixture of both, and neither of them enjoyed it at all.

Next, they couldn't agree on who would have which bedroom in the new house.

"I want the front bedroom," said Luka. "It has the best view."

"No, *I* want the front bedroom," said Harvey. "I like the blue walls."

Luka put his hands on his hips. "Then I want the back bedroom," he said. "It's bigger."

Harvey scowled. "Then *I* want the back bedroom!" he decided. "The red curtains are good for hiding behind."

So, in the end, they agreed to swap rooms every Saturday. It wasn't an ideal solution but, even though both of them were cross, neither boy would back down.

Then they couldn't agree what pet to get.

"A dog!" said Harvey. "Dogs can play football outside!"

"A cat!" said Luka. "They can curl up on your lap when you read."

So, in the end, they didn't get a pet at all, and the arguing didn't stop there.

"It's not fair!" moaned Harvey one evening as his mum was cooking. "Why do we have to have fish fingers?"

"They're Luka's favourite," said Harvey's mum.

"Tomorrow will be your favourite," said Luka's dad. "Meatballs."

"But I HATE meatballs!" said Luka.

"Well, I HATE fish fingers!" said Harvey.

Both boys were just
about to list all the
other things they hated
when the lights went out.
Suddenly, the room was
as dark as night.

Chapter 4: The Power Cut

"What's happening?" wailed Luka's dad.

"It's okay," said Harvey's mum calmly. "It's only a power cut. We just need to get the torches."

"The torches are in the shed," said Luka's dad. He sounded nervous. "I can't go out there in the … dark."

"Well, I can't go," said Harvey's mum. "I need to check on Mrs Hinge next door. She just texted because she's worried. Why don't you boys try to find the torches instead?"

"Okay," said Harvey.

"I suppose," said Luka.

So, off they went into the garden.

The garden was dark, with creatures scuttling in the shadows and leaves whispering in the breeze.

"Are you scared?" asked Luka, trembling.

"Not at all," said Harvey, shivering.

"Maybe we'd better stick together, though," suggested Luka.

"Good idea," said Harvey. "Just in case."

So they did. Together, the boys went to the shed and got the torches, and then pretended they were adventurers making their way home through a deep, dark forest.

When they got inside, Luka's dad had made a picnic tea of fish finger sandwiches, which they ate on the floor on a rug. After that, they attempted to do their homework by torchlight.

"I don't understand this maths!" moaned Harvey.

"I'll help," said Luka. Which was just what he did. For once, Harvey listened and Luka didn't get impatient. Then, when it came to bedtime, they made a big decision.

"Perhaps we could share a room," said Harvey.

"Just for tonight," agreed Luka. "Because of the power cut."

"Great idea," said Luka's dad.

"I'll help move the bed," said Harvey's mum. "Just for tonight."

Chapter 5: Two's Company

Do you know what? The bed never moved back again.

The boys shared the back bedroom, which was bigger. Sometimes, they made complicated dens with sheets and pegs in the front bedroom when they had friends round. (And even when they didn't.)

Luka carried on helping Harvey with his maths homework, while Harvey taught Luka to keep a football in the air for a whole minute.

Best of all, they finally got a pet they could both agree on: a ferret!

"What shall we call him?" asked Harvey.

"I don't know," said Luka.

"Uh-oh," said Luka's dad.

"This doesn't sound good," remarked Harvey's mum.

Fortunately, the boys knew exactly what to do. They each put three names in a hat and got Mrs Hinge from next door to pick one out – because that was the fairest way.

"The ferret's called Horace," declared Mrs Hinge.

"Horace?" said Luka's dad. "What sort of a name is that?"

"Well, I like it," said Harvey's mum.

"Me too," said Harvey.

"Me three," said Luka.

So, the boys went to play with Horace in the garden, leaving their parents to argue over his name.

"Honestly," said Luka as they watched Horace climb in and out of a cardboard box. "Why can't they just agree on things?"

"I don't know," said Harvey. "It's so easy, after all."

Talk about the story

Answer the questions:

1 Which school did Luka and Harvey go to?

2 Whose house did the boys go back to on the first Wednesday afternoon?

3 Why didn't the boys get a pet at first?

4 'Luka snapped back.' What does this phrase tell you about how Luka was feeling? (page 15)

5 Did the way the boys solved the bedroom problem make things better?

6 How did the power cut bring the boys together?

7 What had the boys learned about making decisions fairly by the end of the story?

8 Have you ever had to spend time with someone you don't have much in common with? What happened?

Can you retell the story in your own words?